Franklin's Canoe Trip

From an episode of the animated TV series *Franklin* produced by
Nelvana Limited, Neurones France s.a.r.l. and Neurones Luxembourg S.A.

Based on the *Franklin* books by Paulette Bourgeois and Brenda Clark.

TV tie-in adaptation written by Sharon Jennings and
illustrated by Sean Jeffrey, Mark Koren, and Jelena Sisic.

Based on the TV episode *Franklin's Canoe Trip*, written by Brian Lasenby.

Franklin is a trademark of Kids Can Press Ltd.
Kids Can Press is a Nelvana company.
The character Franklin was created by Paulette Bourgeois and Brenda Clark.

ISBN 0-439-33877-8

12 11 10 9 8 7 6 5 4 3 2 1   2 3 4 5 6/0

Printed in the U.S.A.   23

First Scholastic printing, April 2002

Franklin's Canoe Trip

SCHOLASTIC INC.

New York Toronto London Auckland Sydney

Mexico City New Delhi Hong Kong Buenos Aires

FRANKLIN had been on bus trips with his class and bicycling trips with his friends. He had gone on long car trips with his family. Today, Franklin was going on a canoe trip with his best friend, Bear, and their fathers. Franklin could hardly wait. He wanted to be just like the explorers he had learned about in school.

It was a long drive to Spruce Lake.

"When are we going to get there?" asked Franklin.

"I can't wait to explore," said Bear.

"Maybe we'll discover a whole new country," Franklin added.

Their fathers warned them that canoe trips were hard work.

"We don't mind," said Franklin.

At last, they arrived at the lake. Franklin and
Bear jumped out of the car and ran to the shore.
Bear's father pointed to a big motorboat.

"That sure is a beautiful boat," he said.

Everyone agreed.

"But it's not for explorers," said Franklin.
"Explorers need canoes."

Franklin's father pushed the canoe into the water. Franklin and Bear jumped in.

"Wait!" shouted Bear's father.

But he was too late.

The canoe tipped over, and Franklin and Bear were dumped out.

Franklin's father chuckled.

"First lesson about a canoe is how to get in," he said.

Right side up, Franklin and Bear sat between their fathers, paddles in hand. At first, they kept splashing each other. But they soon figured out the rhythm and were skimming across the water.

"This is fun!" said Bear.

Franklin waved to a motorboat.

"Let's race!" he called.

Everyone laughed.

When they reached the far side of Spruce Lake, Franklin's father got out the map. Franklin and Bear got out lunch.

"Let's take a shortcut and portage to Gull Lake," said Bear's father.

"What's 'portage'?" asked Bear.

His father explained that instead of paddling all the way around the lake, they would carry the canoe overland.

"Just like real explorers!" declared Franklin.

Franklin and Bear led the way. They sang songs and stopped to pick up rocks and pinecones. Then the sun got hotter and hotter, and their backpacks felt heavier and heavier. Before long, Franklin and Bear were trailing behind their fathers.

"Would we have to portage if we had a motorboat?" asked Franklin.

"No," answered his father. "We could get where we're going in two hours in a motorboat. We'd need two days to take the long way in a canoe."

"I wish *we* had a motorboat," Franklin grumbled.

Finally, they reached the shore of Gull Lake. It was rocky and swampy and swarming with mosquitoes.

Franklin and Bear were disappointed.

"Is this it?" asked Franklin.

His father laughed.

"No," he said. "We still have to canoe to Sandy Inlet."

"It's a beautiful deserted beach," added Bear's father. "You can do lots of exploring there."

Franklin and Bear cheered up.

Halfway across Gull Lake, Franklin put down his paddle.

"My arms hurt," he said. "And I'm tired."

"Me, too," said Bear.

"Explorers can't get tired," joked Franklin's father. "*Real* explorers paddled for days without stopping."

Franklin sighed. A motorboat zoomed by, and Franklin sighed again.

By the time they arrived at Sandy Inlet, Franklin and Bear were slumped in the bottom of the canoe.

Several boats were moored in the water, and lots of tents were pitched along the shore.

"Oh, no!" exclaimed Franklin's father.

"It's too crowded to explore," groaned Franklin.

"Come on, Franklin," said Bear. "It's up to us explorers to find a campsite."

Franklin and Bear walked down the beach. Then they climbed the hill at the far end.

And there, in the distance, Franklin saw a tiny perfect cove, with not a boat or tent in sight.

Franklin and Bear ran all the way back and told their fathers about their discovery.

"That's another half hour of paddling," said Franklin's father. "I thought you two were tired."

"Tired?" exclaimed Franklin. "Explorers can't get tired."

They paddled with all their might. Soon the canoe nudged up on a sandbar. Everyone got out to heave it across and into the cove.

"Now I'm glad we *don't* have a motorboat," declared Franklin. "Only canoes can get over this sandbar."

Franklin and Bear helped set up camp, and then
they explored the beach. They drew a map and named
everything they found.

"Let's call this Bear's Lagoon," said Franklin.

"And this is Franklin's Shore," decided Bear.

Soon it was dark. The fire was crackling and fish were frying. Everyone went for a moonlight swim, and they all ate supper listening to the loons.

"There's just one thing left to explore," said Franklin.

And, with a big yawn, he crawled into his sleeping bag.